This Orchard
book belongs to:

_____

_____

_____

To Tigger
G.A.

For my mum and dad
D.W.

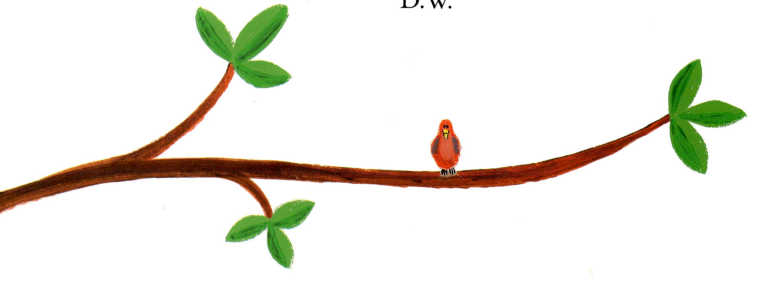

ORCHARD BOOKS
338 Euston Road, London NW1 3BH
Orchard Books Australia
Level 17/207 Kent Street, Sydney, NSW 2000

First published in 1996 by Orchard Books
First published in paperback in 1998
This edition published in 2009
Text © Purple Enterprises Ltd, a Coolabi company 1996 coolabi
Illustrations © David Wojtowycz 1996
The rights of Giles Andreae to be identified as the author and of David Wojtowycz
to be identified as the illustrator of this work have been asserted by them
in accordance with the Copyright, Designs and Patents Act, 1988.
A CIP catalogue record for this book is available from the British Library.

ISBN 978 1 86039 660 1

23 24 25

Printed in China

Orchard Books is a division of Hachette Children's Books,
an Hachette UK company.
www.hachette.co.uk

Rumble in the Jungle

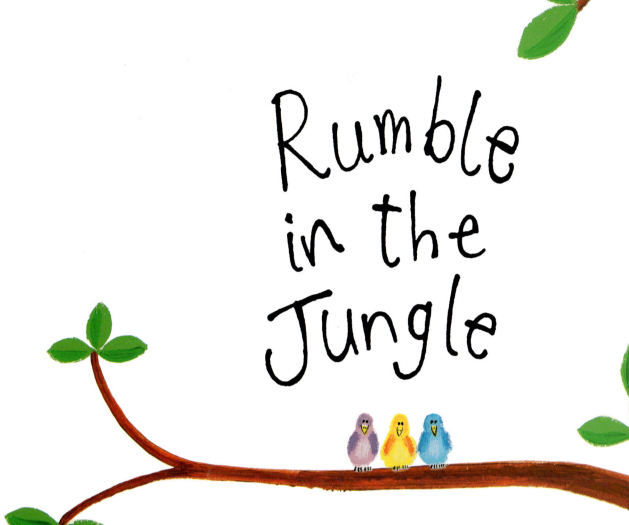

Giles Andreae

Illustrated by
David Wojtowycz

ORCHARD

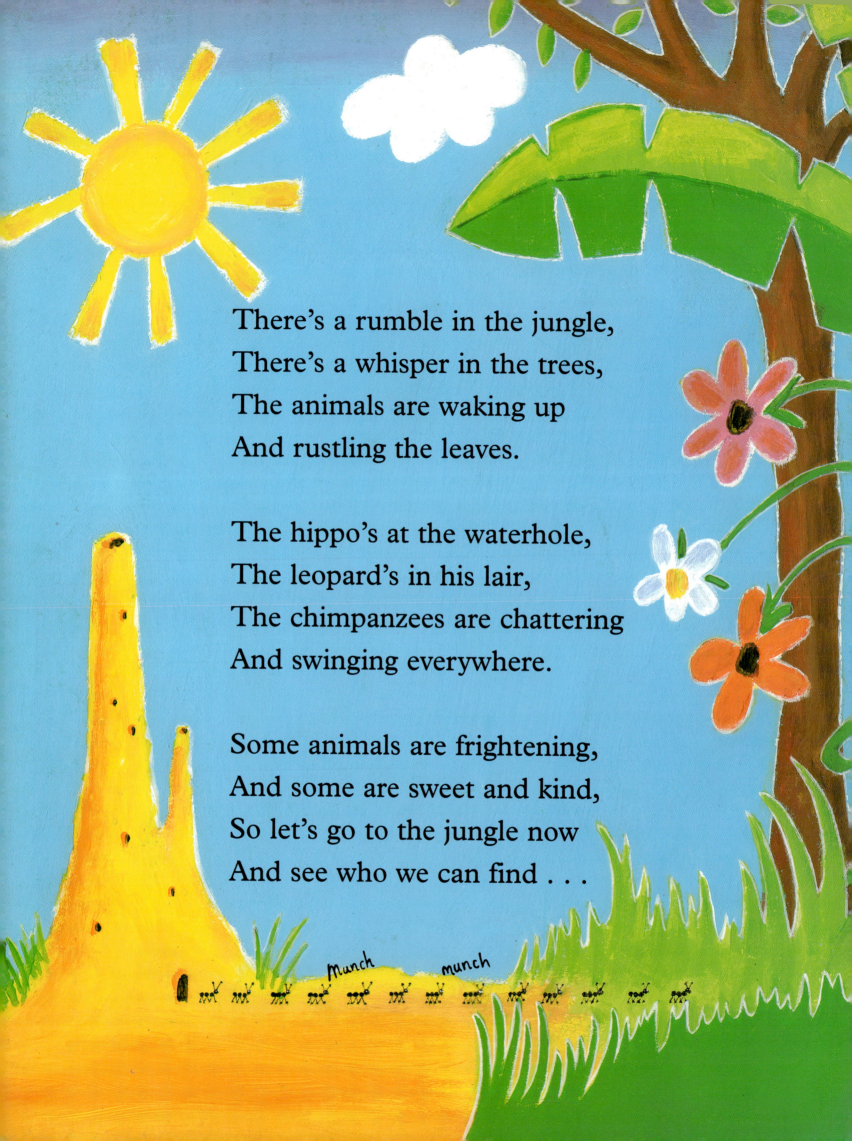

There's a rumble in the jungle,
There's a whisper in the trees,
The animals are waking up
And rustling the leaves.

The hippo's at the waterhole,
The leopard's in his lair,
The chimpanzees are chattering
And swinging everywhere.

Some animals are frightening,
And some are sweet and kind,
So let's go to the jungle now
And see who we can find . . .

munch   munch

And if we can't find nuts to eat

We munch each other's fleas!

Lion

The lion's the king of the jungle
Just listen how loudly he roars!
Every animal quivers
And shudders and shivers
As soon as he opens his jaws.

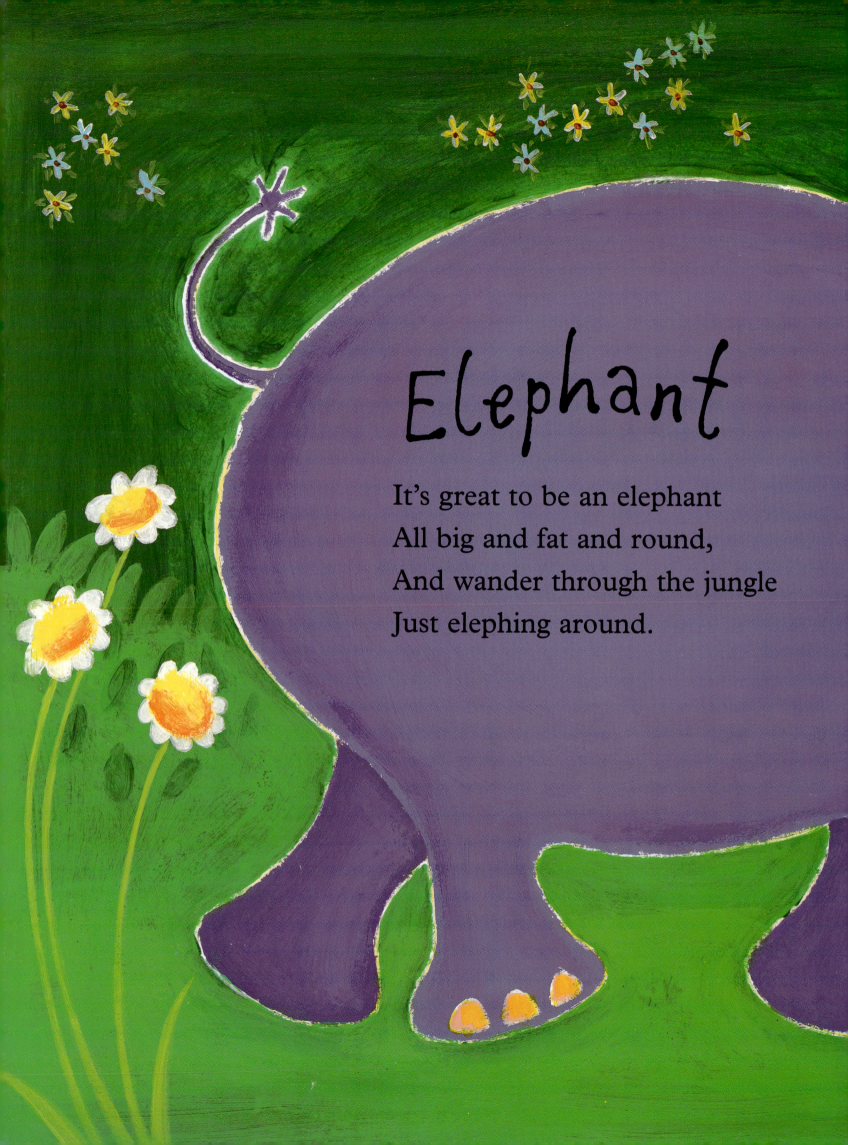

Elephant

It's great to be an elephant
All big and fat and round,
And wander through the jungle
Just elephing around.

munch

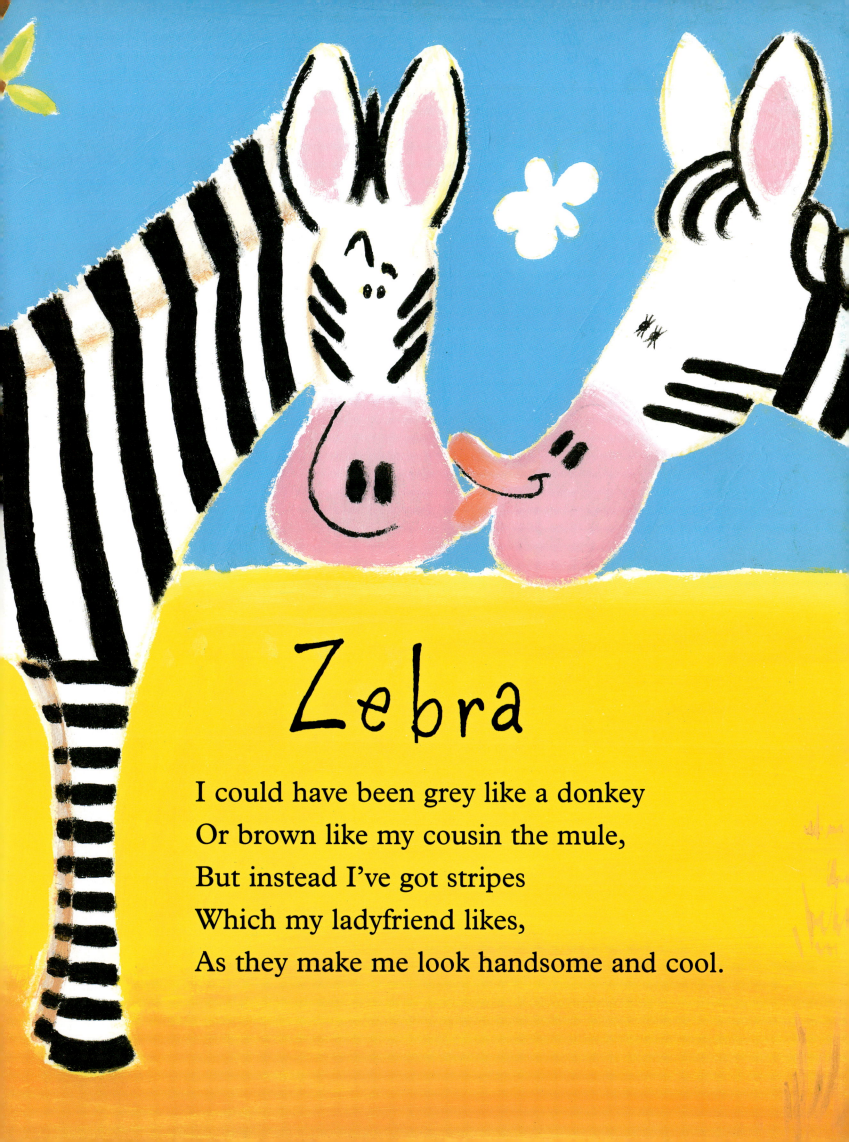

Zebra

I could have been grey like a donkey

Or brown like my cousin the mule,

But instead I've got stripes

Which my ladyfriend likes,

As they make me look handsome and cool.

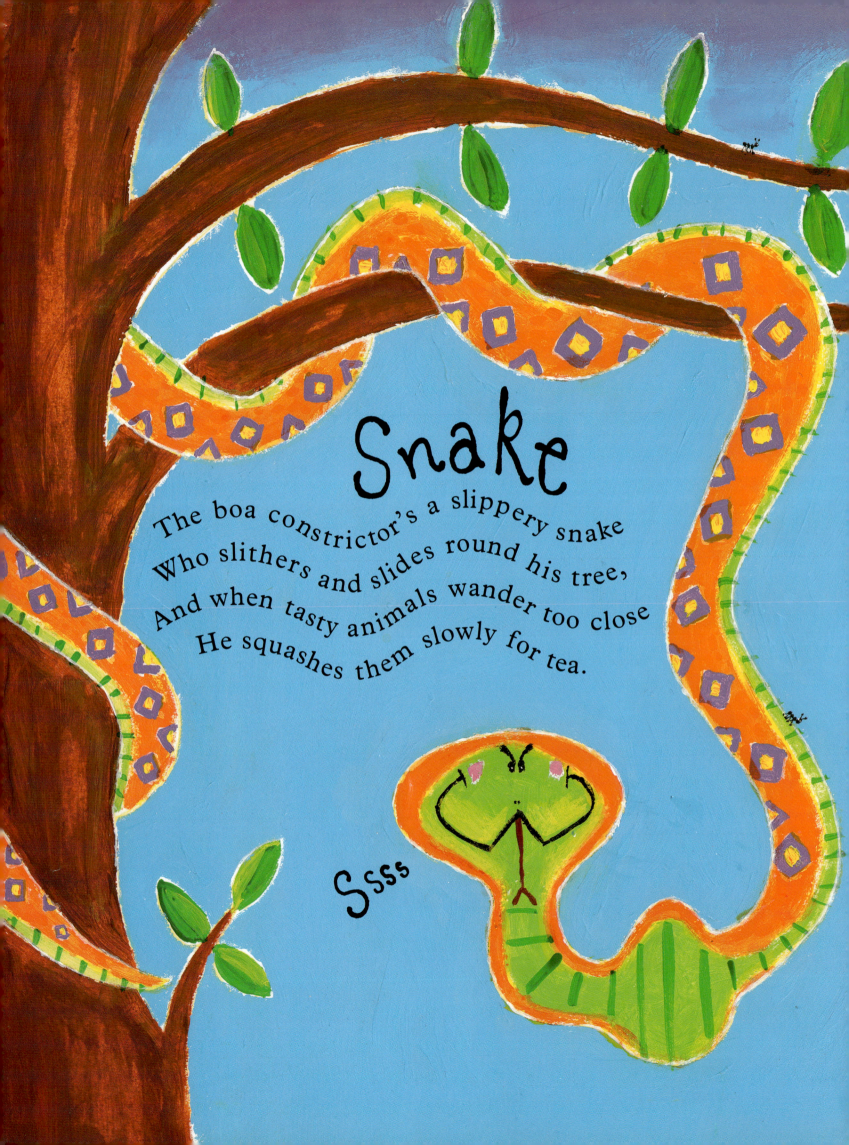

Snake

The boa constrictor's a slippery snake
Who slithers and slides round his tree,
And when tasty animals wander too close
He squashes them slowly for tea.

Ssss

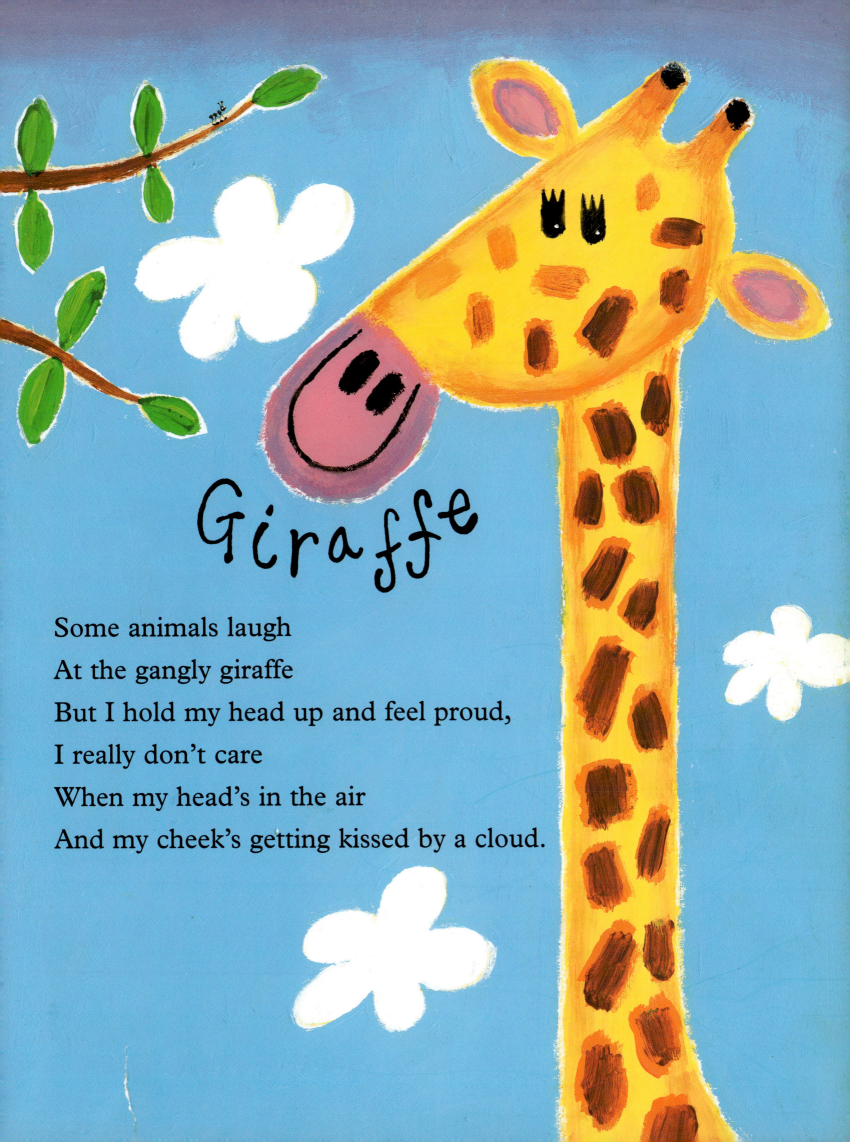

Giraffe

Some animals laugh
At the gangly giraffe
But I hold my head up and feel proud,
I really don't care
When my head's in the air
And my cheek's getting kissed by a cloud.

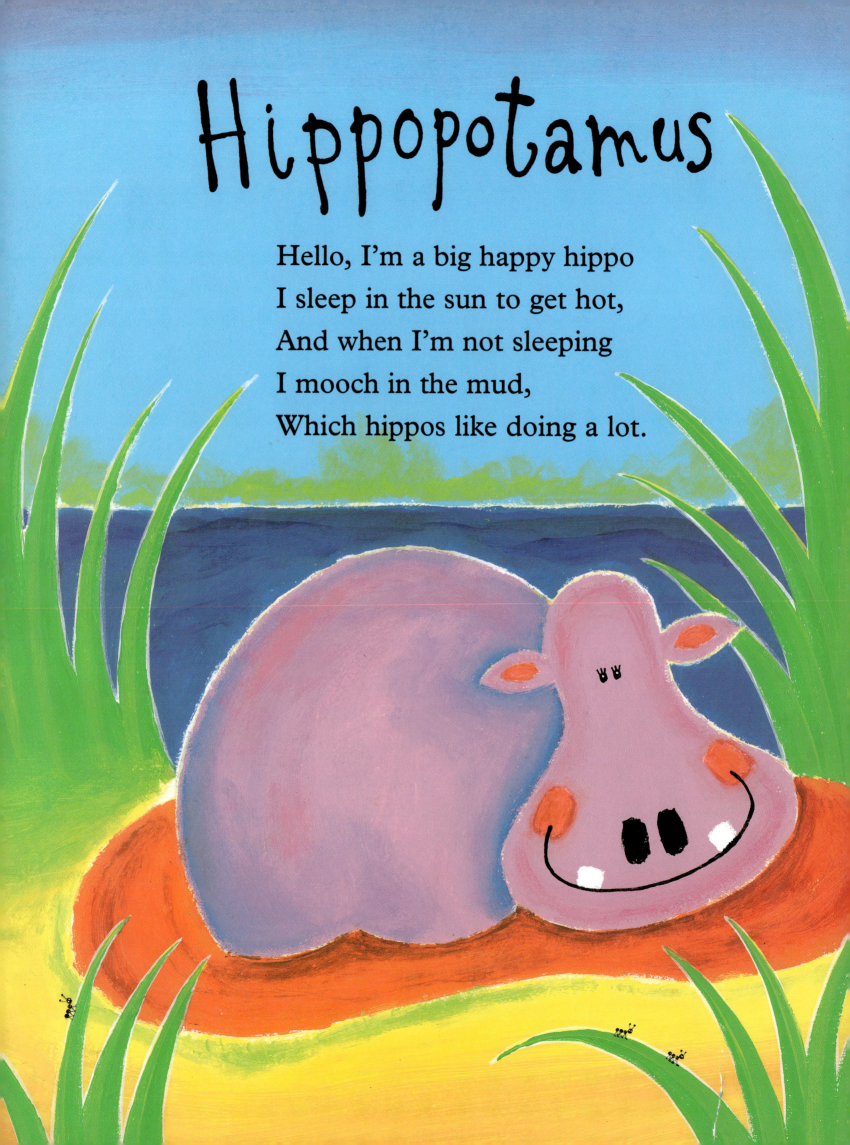

Hippopotamus

Hello, I'm a big happy hippo
I sleep in the sun to get hot,
And when I'm not sleeping
I mooch in the mud,
Which hippos like doing a lot.

Crocodile

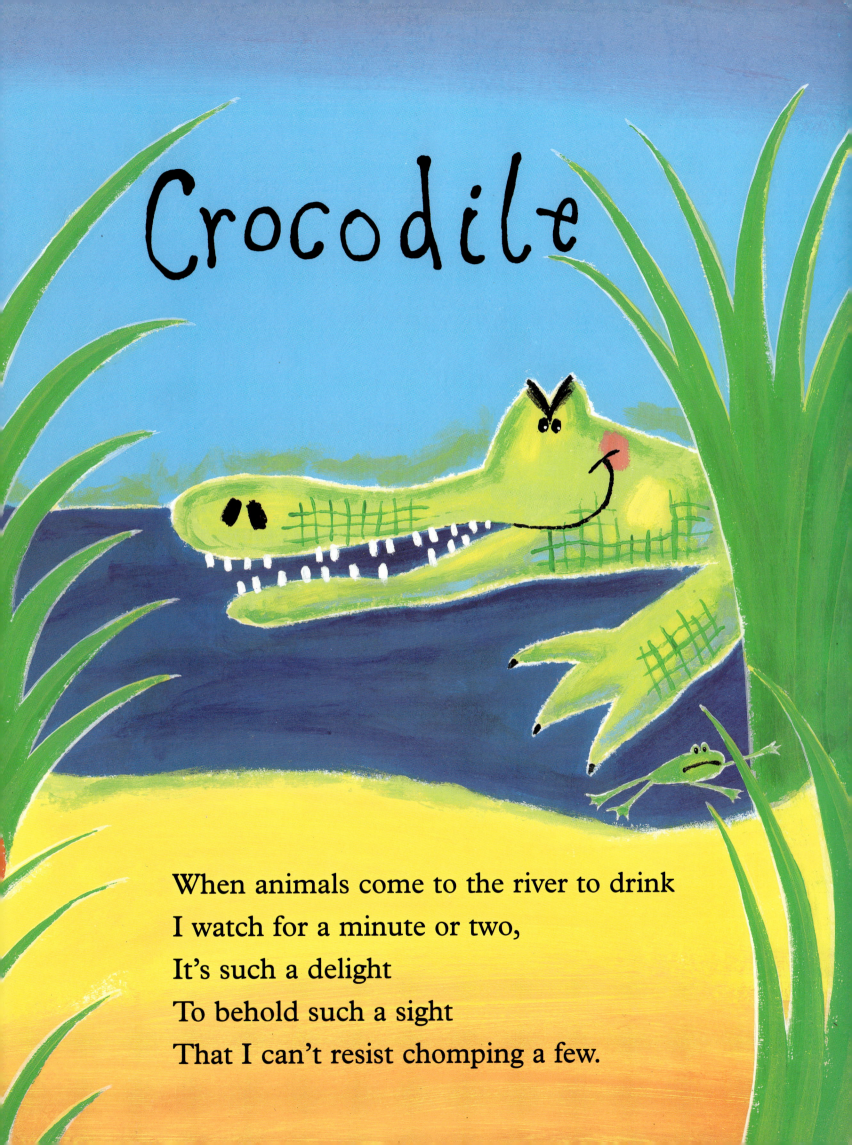

When animals come to the river to drink
I watch for a minute or two,
It's such a delight
To behold such a sight
That I can't resist chomping a few.

Rhinoceros

The ravenous rhino
Is big, strong and tough,
But his skin is all baggy and flappy,
Which means that there's plenty
Of room for his lunch,
And that makes him terribly happy.

Gazelle

No-one can run half as quickly as me
The galloping, gorgeous gazelle,
I can leap up so high
That my horns touch the sky,
And I'm awfully pretty as well.

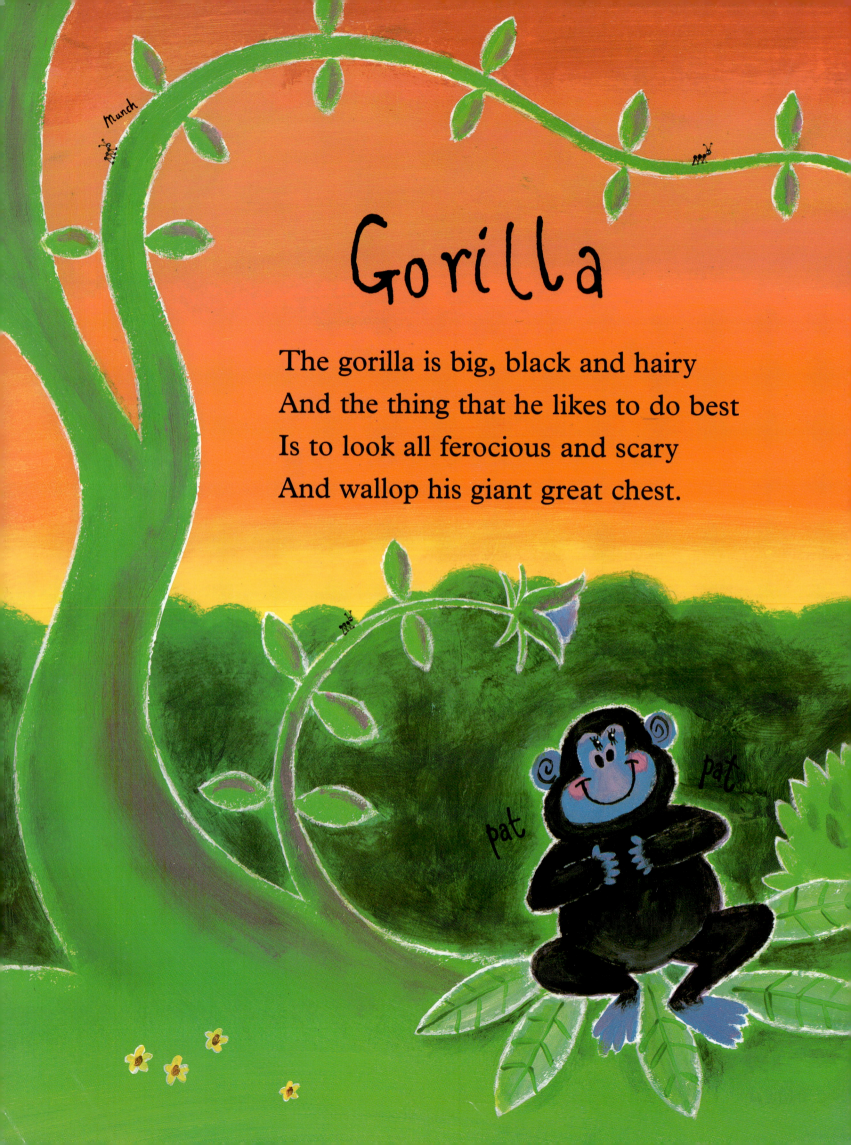

Gorilla

The gorilla is big, black and hairy
And the thing that he likes to do best
Is to look all ferocious and scary
And wallop his giant great chest.

Leopard

If you meet a hungry leopard
Prowling through the night,
Make sure you call him 'Sir'
And be incredibly polite.

Tiger

Beware of the terrible tiger
You don't always know when he's near,
But his eyes shine like lights
Through the blackest of nights,
And his growl makes you tremble with fear.

Grrr

The night has started falling
But the jungle never sleeps,
The vultures circle slowly
While the leopard softly creeps.

And if you listen quietly
You might just hear the growl
Of a hungry pair of panthers,
Who are still out on the prowl.

The lions and their little cubs
Are sleeping in their den,
So let's leave them till tomorrow
When we'll visit them again.